W9-ABT-012

READ IT AND PASS IT ON!

BERNIESBOOKBANK.ORG

THE BEARS GO TO SCHOOL

Kay Winters

illustrated by
Katherine Kirkland

Albert Whitman & Company
Chicago, Illinois

To the bears, who in the spring make their way
to our backyard to raid the bird feeder—K.W.

For the mischievous little bears,
Frazer, Ella, and William!—K.K.

Library of Congress Cataloging-in-Publication Data

Winters, Kay.
Pete & Gabby : the bears go to school / by Kay Winters ; illustrated by Katherine Kirkland.
pages cm
Summary: Pete and Gabby, two curious and rambunctious bear cubs,
leave the park campground and explore a school.
[1. Bears—Fiction. 2. Schools—Fiction. 3. Humorous stories.] I. Kirkland, Katherine, illustrator.
II. Title. III. Title: Pete and Gabby. IV. Title: Bears go to school.
PZ7.W7675Pds 2013
[E]—dc23
2013011300

For more information about Albert Whitman & Company,
visit our web site at www.albertwhitman.com.

The bear cubs, Pete and Gabby,
looked around their empty campground.
"Let's do something **fun**," said Pete.
"We could go exploring," said Gabby.

Off they went.

The cubs trotted along.
Soon they came to a big red building.
Kids were getting out of buses.

"Kids go here!" said Pete.
"This place must be fun!"
The bears crept closer
to get a better look.

A man came out carrying a flag.
Up flew the flag.
Creak…creak…creak.
It flapped in the breeze.

The cubs put their paws over their hearts,
just as they had seen campers do
at the campground.

A bell rang.

The bears stood very still.

What would happen now?

"Maybe we should go inside," said Pete.

"Good idea!" said Gabby.

The cubs opened a back door.

Gabby peeked into a room.
"Look at this!" she said.

Pete banged the drum.
He clanged the cymbal.

Gabby tried the tambourines.
She dinged the triangle.

"This place **is** fun," she said.

"Someone's coming!" said Pete.

"Hide!" said Gabby.

"I thought I heard a drum," a woman said.

"But no one's here." She left.

The cubs looked both ways.
They scampered across the hall.
"Paint!" said Pete. "Like campers
used in the crafts room."

Gabby dipped one paw in red.
She pressed it on the paper.
Pete dipped his paw in blue.

"MMM," he said. "It smells good too."

"Let's do the wall!" said Gabby.
The cubs made paw prints all over
the white wall.

Suddenly Pete knocked over the red paint.
"Careful!" said Gabby, but her paw
hit the yellow.

"OOOPS! Let's get out of here."

They slipped into another room.
The cubs looked around.
This room was **big**!
One wall was covered
with rocks for climbing.

"I can do this," bragged Pete.
Up the side of the wall he went.

"I can go higher!" said Gabby.
She climbed to the very top.

Just then the door opened.
A man wheeled in a cart.

"Freeze," hissed Gabby.
"Look like a rock!"

The man pushed the cart into a closet and left.

"PHEW!" said Gabby. "That was close."
The cubs clambered down.
They heard squawks and squeaks
coming from next door. In they went.

There were small animals in cages.
"Poor things," said Pete.
"It's good we came!" Gabby said.

Science
Room

The cubs opened each cage.

Out hopped the rabbit.

The parakeet flew to the windowsill.

The guinea pig scurried under the teacher's desk.

The hamster trotted to the back of the room.

The snake slithered down the aisle.
Mice skittered every which way.
"We set them free!" Gabby said.
"Like us," said Pete.

Gabby opened the door.

"OHHH," sniffed Pete.

"I'm hungry," he said.

The bears headed toward good smells.

Three women were working
behind a counter.
One was stirring a pot on the stove.
The cubs saw a table with green things.

"OHHH," said Pete. "YUM!"
The bears climbed on the table and munched.
Lettuce,
celery,
peppers,
broccoli.

Pete reached for the spinach.
He knocked over a stack
of salad bowls.

CRASH!

"BEARS!" shrieked a woman.

"Call 911.
Call the police!
Call the park ranger!
Ring the fire alarm!"

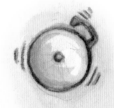

The fire alarm went off.
Children and teachers hurried out
and stood in lines.

"BEARS!" cried the kids, pointing.

The cubs marched out.
They formed their own line.

"KIDS!" cried the bears, waving back.

A police car whizzed in.
A fire truck roared up.
The ranger arrived
on his motorcycle.

"What are the cubs doing here?"
asked the state trooper.
"School is no place for bears!"
"They just like to explore," said the ranger. "Bears will be bears."
"Put them in the back of my cruiser," said the trooper.
"I'll take them back to the park."

"YES!" said Gabby to Pete.
"A siren **and** a flashing light!"
The bears waved good-bye to the children.
The kids waved back.

"Are we in trouble?" Pete asked.

"We're always in trouble," said Gabby.

"But going to school WAS fun!" Pete said.

"Yep!" Gabby grinned. She winked at Pete.

"And as the ranger says…"

"Bears WILL be bears!"